Thar She Blows

Owlkids Books

Chirp, Tweet, and Squawk loved to play in their playhouse. On this particular day, they were playing…

"Pirates!" said Chirp.

"On a pirate ship!" added Tweet.

"With cannons…that go BOOM!" shouted Squawk.

"I'll be Captain Redboots!" said Chirp. "Tweet can be first mate. And Squawk can be the cannon firer."

"Yesss!" said Squawk. "I'll bring the BOOM!"

Thus, Captain Redboots and his trusty crew set sail for a pirate adventure on the high seas.

"All hands on deck!" said Captain Redboots.

"It's time to bring the BOOM!" called Squawk, firing the cannons.

Unfortunately for Captain Redboots and his trusty crew, shuid eat cannonballs!

"Put up the sails!" yelled Captain Redboots.

"But there isn't enough wind," said first mate Tweet.

Captain Redboots and his trusty crew needed something that could make wind for the sails.

"Quick! Look in the treasure chest for something that can help us," said Chirp.

"What treasure chest?" asked Squawk.

"You know!" said Chirp. "Our treasure chest...with all the stuff!"

"Ohhh!" said Squawk. "That box—I mean, treasure chest..."

"It's by the front door," said Tweet. "Let's go get it!"

The three friends opened the lid and looked inside.

"Seashells, popsicle sticks, a sock...Ahoy!" said Chirp as he pulled something out. "This might work!"

"What is it?" asked Squawk.

"It's a fan," said Tweet. "It pulls air in one side and pushes it out the other side even faster!"

"Arrr!" Squawk turned on the fan. Its blades began to spin.

Squawk's pants ballooned in the wind. "Ha-ha! Look! My pants are like a sail!"

"That's it!" said Tweet. "We can use the fan to blow air into the sails!"

Captain Redboots and his trusty crew returned to the ship just as the shuid returned for another attack.

"Thar she blows!" cried the captain. "Quick, mateys! Attach the fan to the ship and point it toward the sails!"

Squawk turned the fan on again.

The sails ballooned in the wind!

"We're saved," cried Tweet.

"Not so fast!" said Chirp. "Shuid like to eat cannonballs, but they LOVE to eat sails!"

Just then, the shuid leaped out of the water and devoured the ship's sails.

"What do we do now?" asked Squawk. "Ships can't sail without sails."

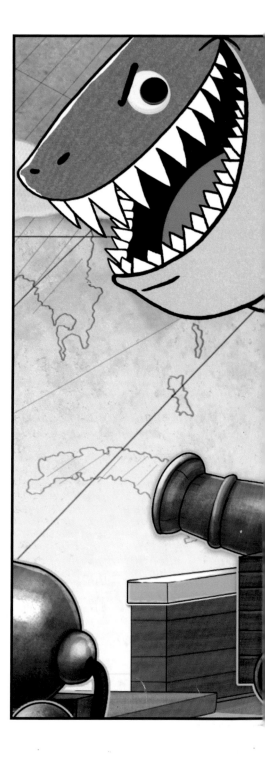

"Wait!" said Tweet. "Lots of boats don't have sails. Some use propellers."

"What's a propeller?" asked Squawk.

"Propellers pull water in one side and push it out the other side even faster," said Tweet.

"That sounds just like a fan," said Chirp. "Except under water!"

"I know what to do," said Squawk. He turned the fan upside down and attached it to the back of the ship.

To the shuid's surprise, the ship took off.

"It worked!" said first mate Tweet.

"Great job, me hearties!" said the captain.

"See you later, alligator...er, I mean, SHUID!" shouted Squawk.

And with that, Captain Redboots and his trusty crew set sail for another famous mission...

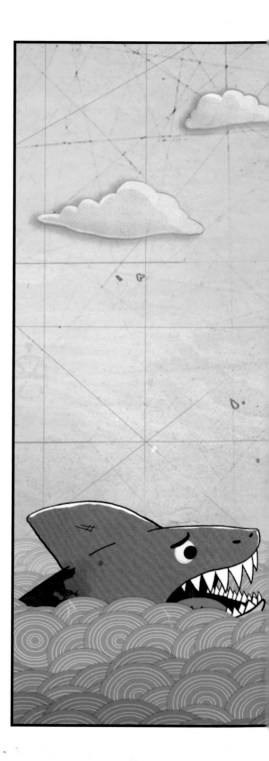

"What's our next mission?" asked Tweet.

"Snack time!" said Chirp. "To the kitchen!"

"Yeah, I'm so hungry I could eat a cannonball!" said Squawk.

From an episode of the animated TV series *Chirp*, produced by Sinking Ship (Chirp) Productions. Based on the Chirp character created by Bob Kain.

Based on the TV episode *There She Blows* written by J.J. Johnson. Story adaptation written by J. Torres.

CHIRP and the CHIRP character are trademarks of Bayard Presse Canada Inc.

Owlkids Books acknowledges the financial support of the Canada Council for the Arts, the Ontario Arts Council, the Government of Canada through the Canada Book Fund (CBF) and the Government of Ontario through the Ontario Media Development Corporation's Book Initiative for our publishing activities.

Published in Canada by
Owlkids Books Inc.
10 Lower Spadina Avenue
Toronto, ON M5V 2Z2

Library and Archives Canada Cataloguing in Publication

Torres, J., 1969-, author
    Thar she blows / adapted by J. Torres.

(Chirp ; 1) Based on the TV program Chirp; writer of the episode: J. J. Johnson.

ISBN 978-1-77147-132-9 (pbk.).--ISBN 978-1-77147-166-4 (bound)

    I. Johnson, J. J., 1980- II. Title. III. Title: Chirp (Television program)

PS8589.O6755667T43 2015   jC813'.54   C2014-908270-3

Edited by: Jessica Burgess
Designed by: Alisa Baldwin

Manufactured in Altona, MB, Canada, in March 2015, by Friesens Corporation
Job #210862

A   B   C   D   E   F

Publisher of Chirp, chickaDEE and OWL
www.owlkidsbooks.com